THE Sister Foxes

ELIZABETH ENLOE

AuthorHouse™
1663 Liberty Drive
Bloomington, IN 47403
www.authorhouse.com
Phone: 1 (800) 839-8640

Published by AuthorHouse 7/17/2018

ISBN: 978-1-5462-5171-2 (sc)
ISBN: 978-1-5462-5172-9 (e)

Library of Congress Control Number: 2018908392

Print information available on the last page.

authorHOUSE®

The Sister Foxes

Written and Illustrated by: Elizabeth Enloe

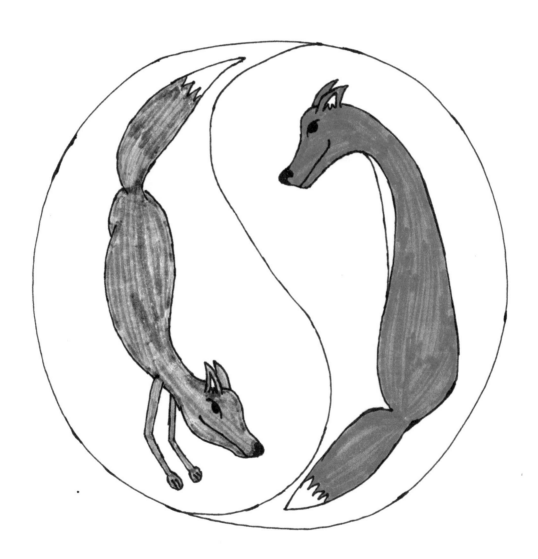

Once upon a time, in two separate forests near a riverbank, there were two sisters.

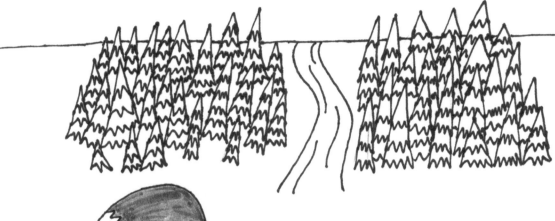

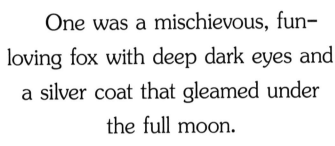

One was a mischievous, fun-loving fox with deep dark eyes and a silver coat that gleamed under the full moon.

The other fox was disciplined, bright eyed rule-follower with a bright-orange coat that reflected the mid-day sun.

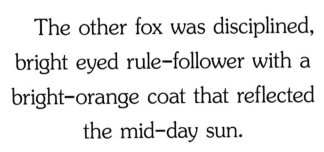

The two were total opposites and, as such, the two sisters kept to themselves in their own sides of the woods. The silver sister lived in the right side of the forest, while the orange fox took the left.

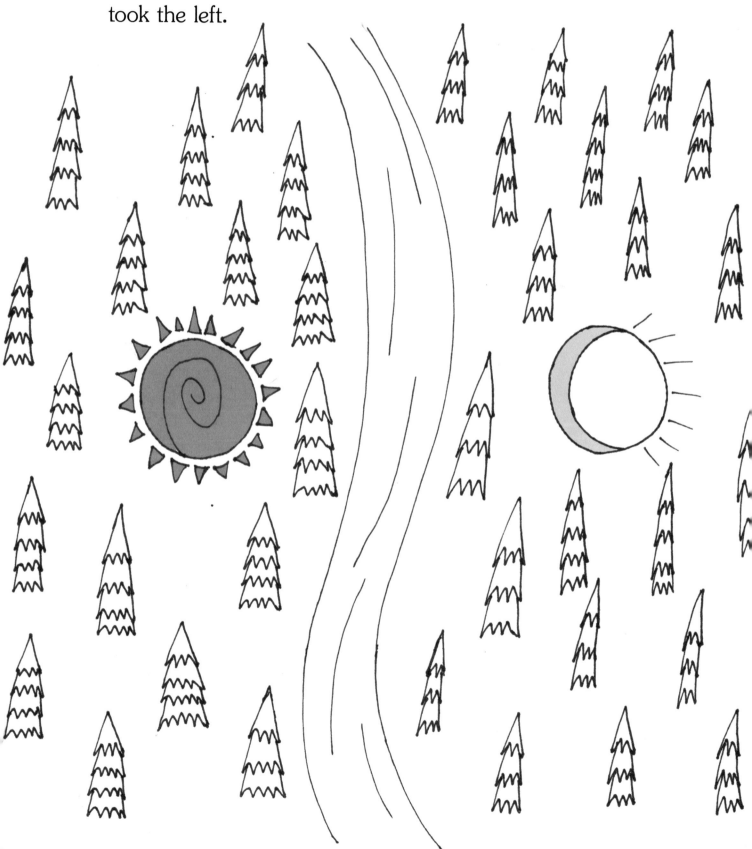

Every night, the silver fox would go up onto the highest rock in her woods and her voice would let loose a song while the moon gleamed down on her silver fur.

"My sister shuns the dark
This place, that is my park
She only seeks the light
I don't share her sight

She takes her light and leave
I have no need to grieve
I live a life of fun and joy
The forest is my private toy

I'm shining bright and clear
I don't care what she hears
But still, down deep inside,
My heart feels like it's being tied.

I just wanna run away
From a life that keeps me in a cage
I don't really need to hear it's fine
Cause I'm still here on my own side!"

Unaware to her, in the separate forest, her sister was singing a song of her own beneath the light of the sun.

"My sister shuns the light
She's just a selfish blight
Her darkness is my curse
I don't dare know worse

She only brings me down
I won't become her clown
These walls keep us apart
I shall stay smart

Perfection and discipline
That is, alone, my goal
Yet still I feel it now,
My empty, blinding soul.
I don't wanna say her name

I don't need to play her games
I am going to stay here and shine
Right here on my only side"

One day, the two sisters were out and about in the thicket of the trees. They both found themselves at the running river of the woods, the boundary that kept their two homes separated. Their eyes met from across the clear water, their distrust for one another being obvious.

"What are you doing here?" The orange fox asked.
"Getting a drink. What else?" the silver fox replied, smirking.
"I wasn't so sure. Forgive me for my lack of trust towards you."
"Meh, doesn't bother me. To be fair, I don't trust you either."
"What? Me? Why not? I never lie."
"That's your problem. You're too trustworthy."
"Says the fox who says nothing but lies!"
"So what?"

The two kept on arguing like that, barking at one another with their hurtful comments.

Until, suddenly...

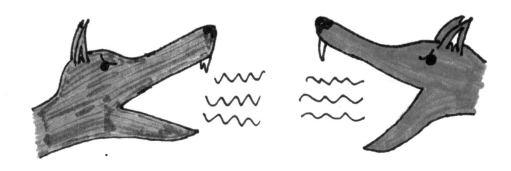

Swoop

Both of the foxes were
snatched up into cages by a
pair of hunters.

Their faces were hidden by a set of darkened masks so the foxes didn't know who was taking them.

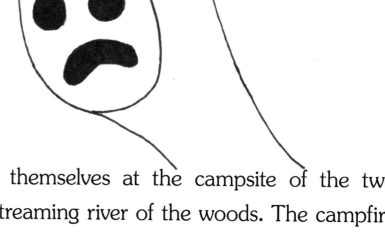

The two sisters found themselves at the campsite of the two hunters, right beside the streaming river of the woods. The campfire at the middle of the site was the only source of light and it made the shadows of the hunters dance along the ground. The two sisters were terrified as their cages stood side-by-side.

"How did this happen?" the orange fox asked herself.

"We had our guard down. That's what happened." the silver fox answered her, "This is why I don't trust humans. How can you trust them?"

"I try to focus only on myself, so they can't get to me."

The silver fox just rolled her darkened eyes.

"Like that's gonna help us here."

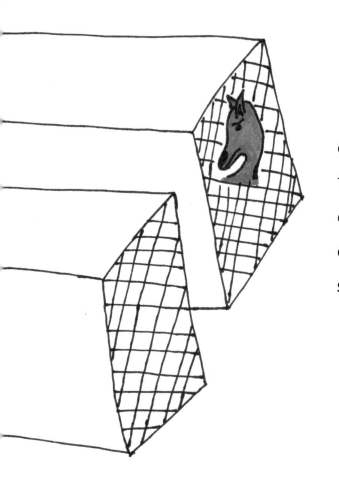

The two sisters remained silent for quite some time, but they both knew that if they were to get out of those cages, they couldn't stay mad at each other forever. The silver fox was still sitting on her cage, her head turned from her twin sister.

"Hey. I don't blame you for blaming humans." the orange fox admitted, "Truthfully, I'm not fond of them either. I just want to stay strong."

The silver fox was surprised, she had never expected the orange fox to admit to something that made her sound so...weak.

"I know that." The silver fox told her, "But I can't stand the thought of humans taking away our forest. I don't blame you for not trusting me. I guess I can be deceitful."

"You think?"

Both of the foxes giggles at each other, the air between them was becoming clearer and clearer with every truthful word.

The silver fox then turned back to the two hunters. The sight of them near the campfire gave her an idea. A rather sneaky idea.

"I think I know a way for us to get out of here. You want to start trusting me, now's your chance. Do you trust me?"

The orange fox was silent, but eventually
answered with a smile.
"Yes. I do."

The hunters didn't pay attention until the cages rattled behind
their backs.

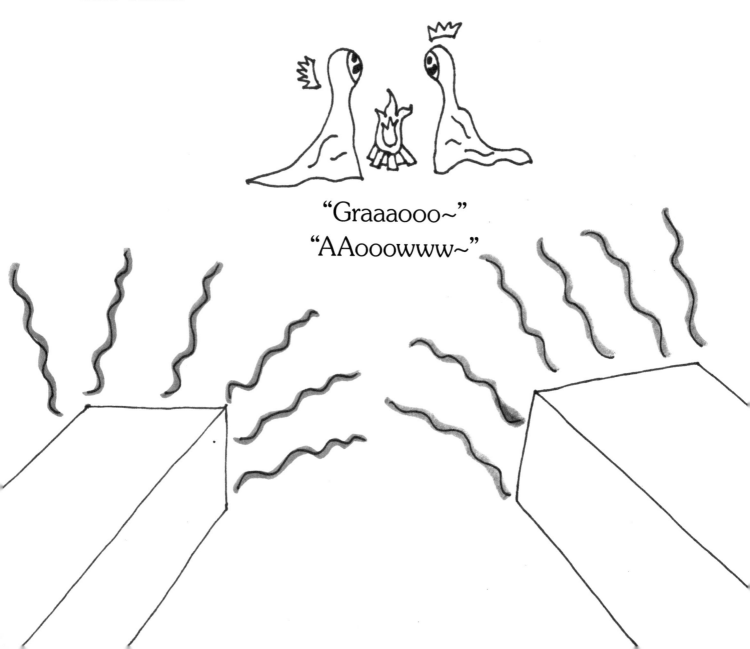

"Graaaooo~"
"AAooowww~"

Whines and cries of pain from the cages caught the hunters attention. The hunters went over and peered through the bars and saw that both the silver and orange foxes were laying on their sides, pretending to be injured. The hunter fell for the twin's act and they opened the cages to check on their animals.

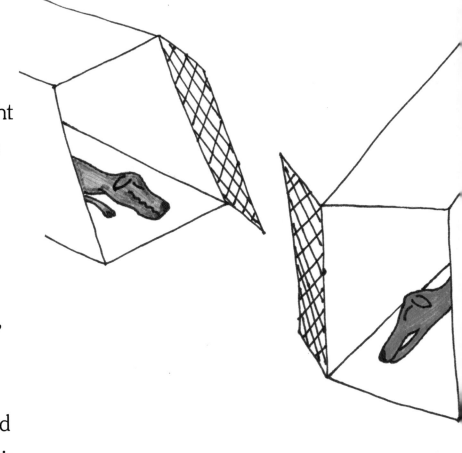

The silver fox used the chance and leap out of the cage with all her might, pushing both of the hunters back with her padded paws as she jumped at them. The two hunters continued to lean back until...

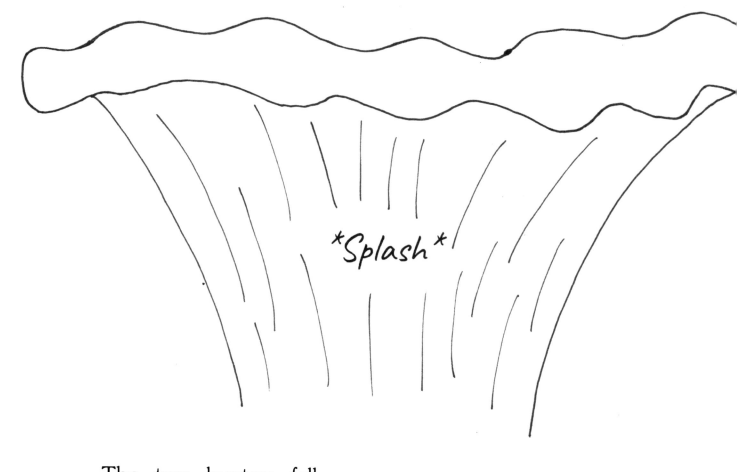

Splash

The two hunters fell right into the river. They squirmed and struggled to swim under the blue waves and the silver fox watched with amusement from the shoreline.

The orange fox stepped out of the cage and saw how her sister watched the hunters try to swim.

"We can't just leave them like that." the orange fox stated, "They'll drown."

"So what? They--"

The orange fox glared at her sister, and the silver one gave in.

"Fine."

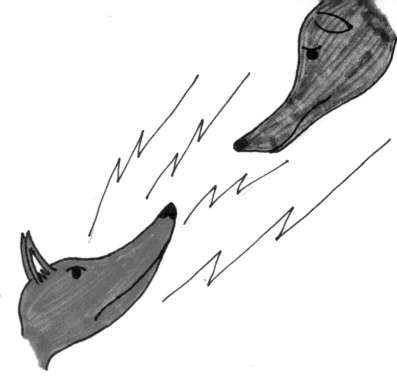

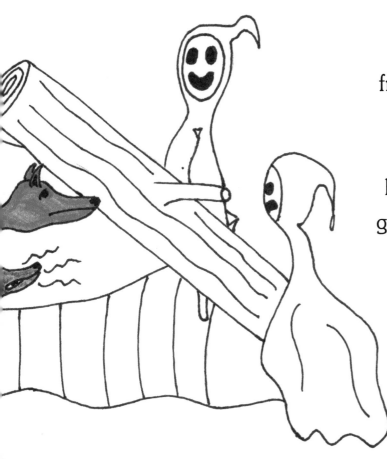

The orange fox smiled and went to grab a nearby branch from the trees that surrounded them. Once she found one, she dragged it to the river, leaning it in for the hunters to grab it. The hunters did so and climbed the branch back onto the ground. The silver fox let out a growl of rage, but the orange fox held her back.

The hunters were relieved when they were out of the river, but the orange fox immediately jumped in front of the two hunters, letting out a fierce roar towards the two.

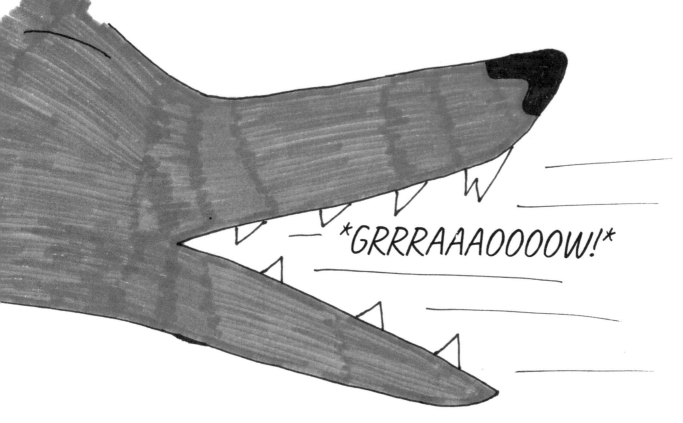

GRRRAAAOOOOW!

The hunters were terrified and ran away from the sisters and out of the woods. The silver fox was shocked at her sister's shout, her muzzle showing a smile of pride.

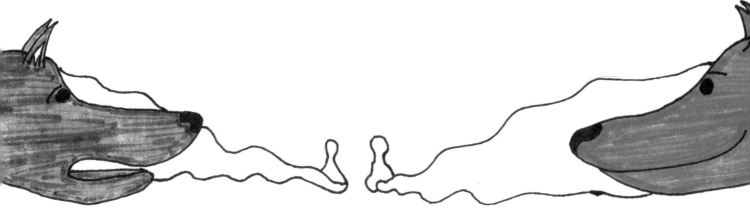

The two sisters made their way back to their own forest borders and stopped once they reached the center of the woods.

"That was fun." The silver fox grinned, "Those hunters were terrified. You're scarier than you look."

"Am not." The orange sister growled, calming down after, "But I never thought I'd be able to trust you. Thank you."

"Meh. Don't mention it." the silver fox gave her sister one final wave with her paw and said, "See ya."

With that, both of the sisters took off towards their own territories. They may have been going two different ways, but they both had the same words in their heads.

"See you soon...Sister."

-The End-

Printed in the United States
By Bookmasters